MW00977384

May you
experience the
joy of Christmas
Many Blessings
Wanda Roone

THIS BOOK BELONGS TO:

_____

CHRISTMAS IS A BIRTHDAY STORY links the lofty throne of heaven with the lowly manger on earth. Wanda Roane gives us unique insights into that fateful night when the powerful hand of the Father touched the tender cheek of the Son in the ultimate act of selfless love.

—Verdun P. Woods, Jr.
Elder, The Potter's House Christian Fellowship, Jacksonville, FL

Get ready to rub the sleep from your eyes on Christmas morning. Wanda Roane's imaginative "Birthday Story" will stir the eyes of your heart to see the wonder of His coming with new clarity and delight! Truly "spiritual meat" for all ages.

—Mark Dobrin

Pastor, Good News Chapel, South San Francisco, CA

Christmas is a Birthday Story
Copyright © 2009 by Wanda Roane. All rights reserved.

This title is also available as a Tate Out Loud product. Visit www.tatepublishing.com for more information.

No part of this publication may be reproduced, stored in a retrieval system or transmitted in any way by any means, electronic, mechanical, photocopy, recording or otherwise without the prior permission of the author except as provided by USA copyright law.

Scripture quotations marked "KJV" are taken from the *Holy Bible, King James Version*.

The opinions expressed by the author are not necessarily those of Tate Publishing, LLC.

Published by Tate Publishing & Enterprises, LLC
127 E. Trade Center Terrace | Mustang, Oklahoma 73064 USA
1.888.361.9473 | www.tatepublishing.com

Tate Publishing is committed to excellence in the publishing industry. The company reflects the philosophy established by the founders, based on Psalm 68:11,
"The Lord gave the word and great was the company of those who published it."

Book design copyright © 2009 by Tate Publishing, LLC. All rights reserved.
Cover and interior design by Elizabeth A. Mason
Illustrations by Kristen Polson

Published in the United States of America

ISBN: 978-1-61566-999-8
1. Juvenile Nonfiction: Holidays & Celebrations: Christmas & Advent
2. Juvenile Nonfiction: Religion: Bible Stories: New Testament
09.06.19

CHRISTMAS
is a
BIRTHDAY STORY

a special story by

Wanda Roane

Tate Publishing & Enterprises

DEDICATION

This book is dedicated in loving memory of my father, George A. Briscoe, and to Dorothy M. Briscoe, my mother and my hero. Thank you for teaching me to pray. Your life and your love inspire me to live to be all that God has called me to be.

ACKNOWLEDGMENTS

To Mark Mitchell, Steve Aurell, and Pat Portman, pastors at Central Peninsula Church: thanks for your encouragement and the opportunity to serve.

Thanks to Mark Dobrin, a minister and friend, who first gave me the opportunity to share *Christmas is a Birthday Story* in a church program.

Thanks to Dora Winn, Jack Bailey, and Marsha Nunley, M.D. You have been a blessing beyond what you can imagine and what can be expressed in words. Thank you for living your faith daily. My life and the lives of my family members have been enriched by the gift of your friendship and talents. Thanks to Kathleen Grant M.D. for all you have done in the care of my mother. She is able to celebrate with me and I am grateful.

Thanks to my sisters, Sandra and Jacqueline, and friends Philip and Bobbi Fagone, for allowing me to share my vision with you and the help and support that you have given me. A special thanks to Elizabeth James, my sister and talented artist, for agreeing to do artwork for this book to help others see the vision.

Thanks to my husband and best friend, Leland. Thank you for understanding my need to do this work and putting up with my early morning writing schedule. I love you forever and always. Thank you to Caleb, my son, for your words of encouragement: "Mommy, I like your book."

The little children are filled with cheer
As Christmas Day is drawing near.

They're filled with stories of Santa Claus
And opening gifts with "oohs" and "ahhs."

Their joy is full, yet not complete
As they run about in stocking feet.

Sampling mother's special treats:
Cookies, cakes, and other sweets.

A turkey's baking through the night,
Holiday food is such a delight.

But what about a spiritual meat,
The yielding of a glory seat?

Because Christmas is a birthday story
Of God's own Son, come down from glory.

Thunderclap and trumpet sound
As heavenly hosts gather around.

God most holy, strong, and true
Announces plans and things to do.

"The time is now, the day has come
To send to them my only Son.

"Go down, Gabriel, take your flight.
Prepare the world for the silent night.

"Visit young Mary, virgin sweet.
I have a promise I must keep."

"Oh, my Son, the one I love,
You must leave heaven above.

"Kneel, my Son, at my feet
And give up your own glory seat.

"Humble yourself by going down
And lay aside your holy crown.

"You're King of kings, your love is true.
You know the plan and what to do!

"From heaven to earth you must go down
And give up your own glory crown."

Cherubim and seraphim
Listen as he speaks with him.

Thou shalt have no other gods before me.

Thou shalt not make unto thee any graven image.

Thou shalt not take the name of the Lord thy God in vain.

Remember the sabbath day to keep it holy.

Honor thy father and thy mother.

Thou shalt not kill.

Thou shalt not commit adultery.

Thou shalt not steal.

Thou shalt not bear false witness.

Thou shalt not covet.

"The man we made has disobeyed.
His debt for sin must be paid.
The blood of bulls and goats won't do,
That's why, my Son, I'm sending you."

"The greatest gift that I can give:
You must die so man can live.
Redemption's plan must unfold,
The greatest love story ever told."

There is silence in heaven all around
As Jesus the Savior prepares to go down.

Kneeling at the mercy seat,
Clothed in a garment down to his feet.

Hair like wool, white as snow,
Eyes like a flame with the brightest glow.

Old
Testament

New
Testament

Greater love has
no one than this,
that he lay down
his life for his
friends.

John 15:13

He looked up to the Holy One.
His face was shining like the sun.

Steps of grace, on feet like brass,
Jesus stood and rose for the task.

His voice was soothing, still and sweet.
Heaven prepared to hear him speak.

The peace that flows from many waters
Filled his voice as he spoke to the Father.

"Oh, my Father, I love you.
I know the plan and what to do.
I'll go to earth. This world I'll save.
I will become a little babe.

"And I'll be there on Christmas Day,
In a manger made of hay.
I'll be the gift you want to give,
And then I'll die so man can live."

"The love I have for man is true,
And this is what I want to do!
I'll take his sins to Calvary.
I'll give my life to make him free!
From heaven to earth I will go down
And give up my own glory crown."

Heaven rejoice and angels sing
Hallelujah to Christ the King!

Jesus left heaven above
And came to give the gift of love.
With his blood, he'll take away sin,
Bring peace on earth, goodwill to men.

Who would have thought a baby boy
Could bring the world so much joy!
All of our praise belongs to him;
He is our Savior and our friend!

As we celebrate this Christmas Day,
Let's think of it in a different way.

Let's feast upon a spiritual meat,
The yielding of a glory seat.

Because Christmas is a birthday story
Of God's own Son come down from glory!

Scriptural Study Guide for

CHRISTMAS IS A BIRTHDAY STORY

"For God so loved the world, that he gave his only begotten Son, that whosoever believeth in him should not perish, but have everlasting life." (John 3:16, KJV)

- Jesus was with God from the beginning. John 1:1–14.
- Man's sin and his need for a Savior. Romans 3:23, 5:8–11, and 6:23.

- The angel's announcement of the coming of Jesus. Luke 1:26–35.
- The awesome description of God and heaven. Isaiah 6:1–8, Revelations 1:10–20.
- The birth of Jesus. Luke 2:1–20.
- The trial, crucifixion, and burial of Jesus. John, chapters 17–19.
- The resurrection of the Lord Jesus. John, chapter 20.

listen|imagine|view|experience

AUDIO BOOK DOWNLOAD INCLUDED WITH THIS BOOK!

In your hands you hold a complete digital entertainment package. Besides purchasing the paper version of this book, this book includes a free download of the audio version of this book. Simply use the code listed below when visiting our website. Once downloaded to your computer, you can listen to the book through your computer's speakers, burn it to an audio CD or save the file to your portable music device (such as Apple's popular iPod) and listen on the go!

How to get your free audio book digital download:

1. Visit www.tatepublishing.com and click on the e|LIVE logo on the home page.
2. Enter the following coupon code:
    7fbe-f48a-367a-bf3b-1e2c-404b-c16e-900b
3. Download the audio book from your e|LIVE digital locker and begin enjoying your new digital entertainment package today!